Clifford's First School Day

Norman Bridwell

SCHOLASTIC INC.

New York Toronto London Auckland

Sydney Mexico City New Delhi Hong Kong

For Deirdre Kathleen

Clifford's First School Day

The author thanks Manny Campana for his contribution to this book.

Ice Cream Mess

Adapted by Josephine Page. Illustrated by Carolyn Bracken and Steve Haefele.
From the television script "Screaming for Ice Cream" by Sheryl Scarborough and Kayte Kuche.

This special edition was printed in 2011 for Kohl's Department Stores, Inc.
(for distribution on behalf of Kohl's Cares, LLC, its wholly owned subsidiary) by Scholastic Inc.

Kohl's
0-545-35122-7
123386
04/11

ISBN 978-0-545-35122-5

10 9 8 7 6 5 4 3 2 1 11 12 13 14 15 16/0

Printed in China 127
This edition printing, May 2011

I'm Emily Elizabeth. Every day I ride to school on my dog Clifford. Clifford is too big to go inside.

Clifford hasn't been inside a school since he was a tiny puppy.

I took him one day for show-and-tell.

All the kids wanted to pet my very tiny puppy. Miss Pearson liked him, too, but she said it was time to begin our day.

First she put out the finger paint. I love finger painting.

Clifford got right up on the table.

He sniffed the yellow paint.

Oh my. The jar tipped over!

Clifford found out that paint is very slippery.

Miss Pearson said Clifford was a good artist.

He made a beautiful yellow picture.

We couldn't leave Clifford all covered with paint. Miss Pearson thought that some water play might be a good way to get him clean.

Tim had made a boat out of a milk carton.
Clifford was a perfect captain for the boat.

Captain Clifford climbed the mast
to look around . . . .

And that's how we got the paint off.

Miss Pearson dried him off. She said we were going to make cookies next and Clifford could watch. That would keep him out of trouble.

While Miss Pearson rolled out the cookie dough,
Clifford got curious about the bag of flour.

FLOUR

Ooops!

Clifford made another mess.

Miss Pearson said it might be a good idea for Clifford to play outside. We all went out to the playground.

I thought Clifford would enjoy the slide.

He wiggled out of my hands . . .

. . . and went down the slide by himself.

He landed in the sandbox.

We helped the kids rebuild their sand castle.

We made Clifford the king of the castle.

He loved that.

Then it was lunchtime.

I shared my sandwich and dessert with Clifford.

He gobbled up his sandwich.

But he didn't know how to eat the dessert.

Poor Clifford chased the wiggly cubes all over the floor.
The other kids thought that was funny.

Miss Pearson said it was time for Clifford to go home and have a real lunch. She told me to bring him back to school when he was a little bigger.

She should see him now.

Clifford's
Ice Cream Mess

Clifford's
Ice Cream Mess

SCHOLASTIC INC.
New York Toronto London Auckland
Sydney Mexico City New Delhi Hong Kong

Hi! I'm Emily Elizabeth, and I have a dog named Clifford. One hot summer day, my friend Charley and I were playing trash-lid hockey.

Clifford played, too! Cleo and T-Bone cheered him on.

Just then, Charley's dad called to us. He owned the Snack Shack. "I'm closing the store for a while," he said. "If you need anything, just go next door to Ms. Kit. She'll help you."

And off he went.

"I'll make you an ice-cream cone," Charley said to me.

I wasn't sure if Charley was allowed to operate the ice cream machine, but it was an awfully hot day, and Charley seemed to know what he was doing.

Just then, a tourist came by. “I’ll have an ice-cream cone, too,” he said.

“Sure thing,” Charley said to the tourist.

“It’s okay,” Charley said to me. “I help my dad all the time.”

It was true that Charley helped his dad while his dad was there. But this was different. And I was beginning to worry.

More tourists came by, all wanting ice-cream cones.

So Charley and I made the cones, Cleo served them, and T-Bone collected the money.

But something went wrong. “I can’t stop the machine,” Charley said.

All the tourists had gone away by then.

"Eat fast," Charley said. But we couldn't eat fast enough to keep up with the machine. By that time, we were knee-deep in ice cream.

I think T-Bone was frightened. He jumped up on a crate and wouldn't come down.

The machine was making more and more ice cream. Soon I was up to my waist in the stuff.

I thought Charley should go to Ms. Kit for help. But Charley wanted to handle things himself.

Meanwhile, the dogs seemed to be having a grand old time. Cleo and T-Bone used trash can lids to surf the ice cream. Clifford blew the ice cream and made big waves for them.

T-Bone seemed to have gotten over his fear pretty quickly!

But Charley and I weren't having any fun at all. We were up to our chests in ice cream—and in deep, deep trouble.

"I wish I knew how to fix this," Charley said.

“I can fix it,” said Charley’s dad.

He maneuvered the lever, and the machine stopped. But it was too late. Ice cream was everywhere.

"You should have asked Ms. Kit for help," Charley's dad said.

Charley felt very ashamed. "Sorry, Dad," he said. "I really thought I could handle it."

On that day, Charley and I learned an important lesson—if you need help, ask for it.

Charley's dad gave each of us a mop, and together we cleaned that big ice cream mess.

The dogs helped, too. T-Bone and Cleo ate until they couldn't eat any more.

But Clifford still had room for one last lick!